Rip Van Winkle
by Washington Irving
Retold and illustrated by John Howe

Little, Brown and Company
Boston   Toronto

For my wife, Fataneh, who also loves sleeping in

First Edition

Library of Congress Cataloging-in-Publication Data
Howe, John, 1957–
    Rip Van Winkle.

    Summary: A man who sleeps for twenty
years in the Catskill Mountains wakes to a much-
changed world.
    [1. Catskill Mountains region (N.Y.)—Fiction.
2. New York (State)—Fiction] I. Irving, Washington,
1783–1859. Rip Van Winkle. II. Title.
PZ7.H83737Ri 1988   [E]   86-21107
ISBN 0-316-37578-0

NIL
*Published simultaneously in Canada
by Little, Brown & Company (Canada) Limited*

Printed in Italy

The Catskill Mountains are full of magic and legends. They swell up to a noble height above the Hudson River and seem to change color and shape with the change of season and weather. The old stories say that the spirits of Henry Hudson, his crew, and the first Dutch settlers still walk along the crags and valleys of these remarkable mountains.

At the foot of the Catskills is a little village founded by some of those first colonists. In this village there lived a simple, good-natured fellow by the name of Rip Van Winkle.

The people of the village all loved Rip, and some believed that he owed his good nature to his troubles at home. For it is said that men who are wed to shrews are often the most pleasant when away from home, and Rip was a henpecked husband.

If Rip's wife often greeted him with a frown, the children of the village would shout with joy and laughter whenever he approached. Rip took part in their sports, taught them to fly kites and shoot marbles, and he told them long stories of ghosts and witches. Whenever he went walking about the village, he was surrounded by a troop of these children, and not a dog in the village would bark at him.

The great fault in Rip's makeup was his dislike for profitable work. He sometimes sat on a wet rock all day long and fished, even though he felt not one single nibble. And he would never refuse to help a neighbor. Indeed, the women of the village used him to run errands and do the odd jobs their husbands would not do for them. In a word, Rip was ready to do anyone's business but his own.

Rip declared, however, that it was easier to help others than to keep his own farm in order. Everything there went wrong, he said, despite his best efforts. His fences were always falling to pieces; weeds were sure to grow in his fields more quickly than anywhere else, and the rain always began to fall just as he was about to start some outside work.

His children, too, were ragged and wild. His son, Rip, seemed to inherit his father's habits along with his old clothes. He was generally seen trotting around like a colt, holding up a pair of his father's cast-off trousers with one hand as a fine lady does her skirts in bad weather.

Yet Rip Van Winkle was one of those happy people who take the world at ease, who would rather starve on a dime than work for a dollar, and, if left to himself, Rip would have whistled his life away quite happily.

This behavior enraged his wife. She continually complained about his laziness and the ruin he was bringing on his family. Morning, noon, and night her tongue was incessantly going, and everything Rip did or said was sure to produce a torrent of abuse. In answer Rip shrugged his shoulders, rolled his eyes but said nothing. This would only make his wife angrier. Rip's only way to escape from the labor of the farm and the abuse of his wife was to take his old matchlock, call his dog, Wolf, to his side, and go for a stroll in the woods.

One fine autumn day Rip went out after his favorite sport, squirrels, and the Catskill Mountains echoed with the reports of his gun and Wolf's excited barking. Late in the afternoon, panting and fatigued from the hunt, Rip threw himself on a green knoll. In the distance he saw the lordly Hudson moving on its silent, majestic course, and for some time he looked at this scene. Evening gradually approached; the mountains threw their long blue shadows over the valley, and Rip saw it would be dark long before he reached the village. He heaved a deep sigh when he thought of what his wife would say when he was late coming home.

Then, as he was about to descend from the mountain, he heard a voice in the distance: "Rip Van Winkle! Rip Van Winkle!" He looked around but could see nothing.

He thought his ears must have deceived him, and turned again to descend when he heard the same cry ring through the still evening air: "Rip Van Winkle! Rip Van Winkle!"

Wolf bristled and bared his teeth and, giving a low growl, he skulked by his master's side. Rip felt a vague fear creep over him. He looked anxiously in the direction from which the cry had come. A strange figure slowly climbed up the path, bent under the weight of something he carried on his back. Rip was surprised to see any human being in this lonely place, but, thinking the man might need his help, he walked toward him.

As Rip came closer he was still more surprised at the stranger's appearance. He was a short, squarely-built old fellow with thick, bushy hair and a gray beard. His dress was of an antique Dutch fashion, and he carried a big keg that seemed full of liquor. He did not speak, but he made signs for Rip to approach and help him with the load. Though distrustful of this strange man, Rip helped him, and they took turns carrying the heavy keg as they silently climbed up a narrow gully.

As they went along Rip every now and then heard long rolling peals, like distant thunder, that seemed to come from a deep ravine between the rocks above them. He paused for a moment, but supposing the sound to be the muttering of one of those thunderstorms that often take place in the mountains, he went on.

They finally came to a small circular hollow, and when they entered, Rip saw a company of small men playing at long pins. What a strange group they were! One had a large beard and small piggish eyes. The face of another seemed to consist entirely of nose, and he wore a tall gray hat set off with a pink feather. They all had beards of various shapes and colors, and the longest one belonged to the one who seemed to be the commander. He was a stout old gentleman with a weather-beaten face.

Rip greeted them politely, but they answered not a word. Nothing, indeed, interrupted the stillness of the scene but the noises of the balls. When they were rolled, they echoed along the mountains like rumbling peals of thunder.

Rip and his companion came closer. The men suddenly stopped their play and stared at him in a way that made his heart flip within him and his knees knock together.

His companion now emptied the contents of the keg into two large flagons and made signs indicating that Rip should pass these flagons among the players. He obeyed with fear and trembling. The strange little men drank down the liquor in absolute silence and returned to their game.

Since the men did not seem to mean him harm, Rip's fear began to leave him. He even took a sip for himself from one of the flagons when no one was looking. Rip found he liked the taste of the strong liquor and he soon stole another sip, and then another, until he became dizzy. His eyes swam in his head and then closed; Rip fell into a deep sleep.

When Rip awoke he found himself on the spot where he had first seen the old man with the keg. He rubbed his eyes. "Surely," said Rip aloud, "I have not slept here the whole night." Then he remembered what had happened the night before: the strange men, the kegs, the mountain hollow, the game of ninepins, and the flagon. "Oh, what have I done?" thought Rip. "What excuse shall I make to my wife? I cannot tell her of my adventure. She will never believe me."

He looked around for his gun, but in place of his clean, well-oiled piece he found an old rifle lying beside him, the barrel rusted, the stock worm-eaten, and the lock falling off. He suspected that the old men had stolen his rifle, and he became determined to find them and demand what was his. He whistled for Wolf and got to his feet. Wolf did not come running, and when Rip rose, he found himself stiff in the joints. "These mountain beds do not agree with me," he mumbled, and he began to return to the hollow where he had last seen the men playing ninepins.

He soon found that he could not retrace his steps. Brambles and trees must have grown quickly overnight, for they blocked his way. What was he to do? He sat down to think, and the morning passed away. Rip began to feel very hungry, so he finally decided to give up his gun and go face the anger of his wife. He whistled for Wolf, and when the dog still did not appear, Rip turned and slowly started homeward.

As he approached the village, he met a number of people, none of whom he knew. That surprised him, for he thought he knew everyone in the village. These people dressed strangely and when he passed they stared at him and stroked their chins. This repeated gesture made Rip stroke his chin too. He gasped in surprise, for he found that his beard had grown a foot long!

When Rip entered the village, everything there was strange to him. A troop of strange children ran at his heels; strange dogs barked at him; unfamiliar faces were at the windows and on the streets, and unknown names were over the doors. Rip began to be afraid. Was he bewitched? Surely this was not the village he had left the day before.

With some difficulty he found his way to his own small farm. He expected at any moment to hear the scolding voice of his wife, but silence greeted him. The house was in ruin. Its roof had fallen in, and a half-starved dog that looked a bit like Wolf skulked about it. When he called out his wife's name, his voice echoed briefly for a moment, then silence fell again.

Rip hurried back to the village to find the inn. Surely friends would be gathered there—but it too was gone. In its place was a tall pole with a strange striped flag fluttering from it.

As Rip stood and stared at the flag, a crowd of villagers gathered around him. They eyed him with curiosity. Soon one short, stout man bustled up to him and began to ask him questions. "Tell me, sir, who are you? Did you fight in the revolution? Where do you come from?" Rip stared blankly at him, for he hadn't the slightest idea what the man was talking about. Finally he cried out, "Does nobody here know Rip Van Winkle?"

"Oh, to be sure," said one of the bystanders. "There he is leaning against that tree."

Rip looked and saw a double of himself, just as he had looked when he went up the mountain. He was now completely confused, and when the short, stout man again asked him his name, he couldn't answer for a moment. Then he said, "I am not sure. I was myself when I fell asleep last night, but now they've stolen my matchlock and nothing seems the same."

The bystanders now winked at one another and tapped their fingers against their foreheads. They thought Rip was crazy.

At that very moment a young woman passed through the crowd with a baby in her arms. "Hush, Rip," she said to the child, "the old man won't hurt you." The name of the child and something about the young woman's manner made Rip pause. "What is your name, my good woman?" he asked.

"Judith Gardiner," was the answer.

"And your father's name?"

"Ah, poor man, Rip Van Winkle was his name, but it's twenty years since he went away from home, and never was heard of since. His dog came home, but I and my brother, who stands under yonder tree, have never seen our father since that day."

Rip then asked in a faltering voice, "And what happened to your mother?"

"Oh, she died a short time after my father disappeared. She broke a blood vessel in a fit of anger at a New England peddler."

Rip could be quiet no longer. "I am your father!" he cried. "Young Rip Van Winkle once. Old Rip Van Winkle now. Does no one recognize me?"

The people were astounded by Rip's words. Finally an old woman tottered out of the crowd, looked carefully and then declared, "Sure enough, it is Rip Van Winkle! Welcome home, old neighbor. Where have you been for the past twenty years?"

Rip soon told his story. The whole twenty years had passed as if they had been one night. Some of the villagers believed him; others still thought him crazy, and when the crowd broke up, Rip's daughter brought him home to live with her. She had a snug house and a cheerful husband, and Rip soon settled in nicely with them.

Rip returned to his old habits. He took long walks and made new friends. He often paused at the new village inn and told his amazing story to every stranger who arrived in the village. Some doubted the truth of it, but the old Dutch inhabitants, who knew the old legends, came to believe it. Many henpecked husbands have been heard to say they wish that they, too, might have a long drink out of Rip Van Winkle's flagon. And even to this day they never hear a summer thunderstorm in the Catskills without saying that Henry Hudson and his crew are playing their game of ninepins.